D0352861

For Sadie and the Nurses of Ward 3

A Sparrow Book
Published by Arrow Books

An imprint of the Hutchinson Publishing Group

London Melbourne Sydney Auckland Wellington Johannesburg
and agencies throughout the world

First published by Andersen Press 1978
Sparrow edition 1981
Text © Bernard Stone 1978
Illustrations © Ralph Steadman 1978
All rights reserved

ISBN 0 09 926630 X

Emergency Mouse

A Story by Bernard Stone

Illustrated by Ralph Steadman

A Sparrow Book

It was midnight. The ward was dark and quiet. All the patients were sound asleep—except for Henry.
He was in hospital for an operation. His bed was very comfortable and warm, but the pain in his jaw was keeping him awake.

He tried to think of all the things he liked doing best.

Then he remembered his pet mouse, Whitey. On the day Henry had come into hospital, the mouse had been very sick. Henry did hope that his mother was keeping a watchful eye over him.

Henry missed his mother. He turned over on his side and tried to go to sleep. Just as he was closing his eyes, he noticed several tiny lights above little doors in the skirting board.

Suddenly the doors opened and mice dressed as doctors and
nurses wheeled out a lot of little beds and pushed them into rows.
Henry couldn't believe his eyes—he leant over the edge of his bed
to get a closer look.

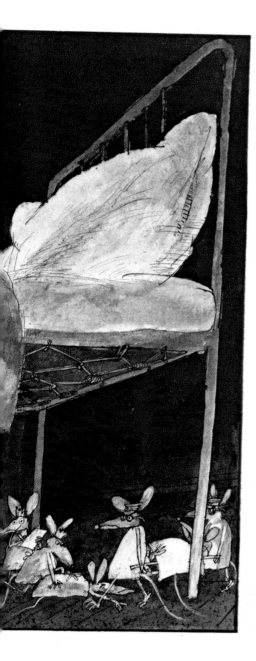

The mice were taking over the hospital for the night, setting up their own ward with a mouse surgeon and doctors and nurses to take care of all the mouse patients.

There was Fatty Mouse, who naturally was over-weight. He was put on a liquid diet and the doctor said he would soon be much thinner.

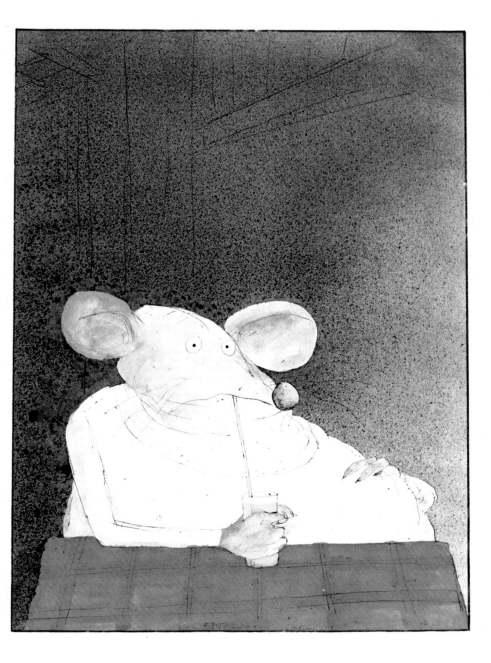

In the next bed was Toothy Mouse. He had raided a sweetshop and was now waiting to see the dentist.

Poor Limping Mouse hadn't been quite quick enough and had been caught by a cat. But he was making good progress learning to walk with crutches.

Tropical Mouse had stowed away on a ship from foreign parts. He was suffering from a rare tropical disease. He was the yellowest mouse you ever saw.

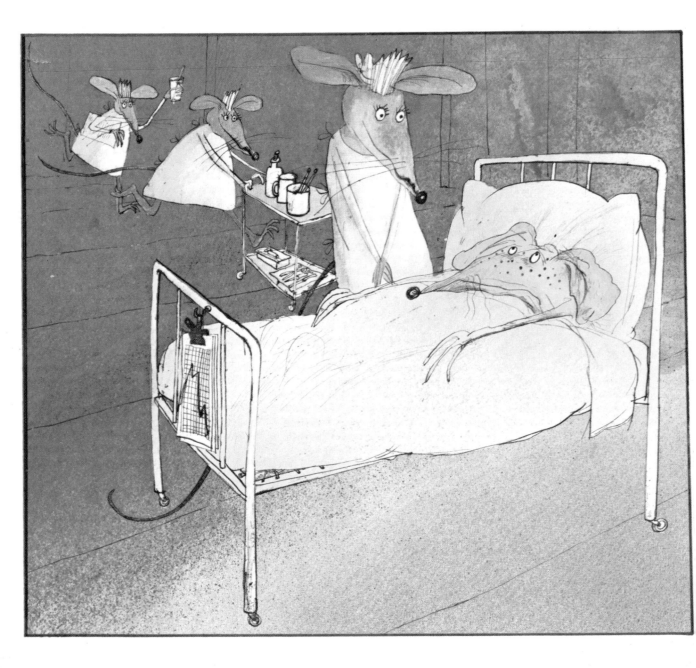

Fuss-Pot Mouse was back again. He was always in and out of hospital. He thought he had every illness in the medical dictionary. The doctors let him stay a few days each time and then sent him home.

"Emergency here! Get him to the operating theatre at once!" It was Surgeon Mouse speaking. Champion Mouse, the daredevil cheese-stealer, had been caught in the act at last and he was brought in with a mouse-trap firmly gripping his tail.

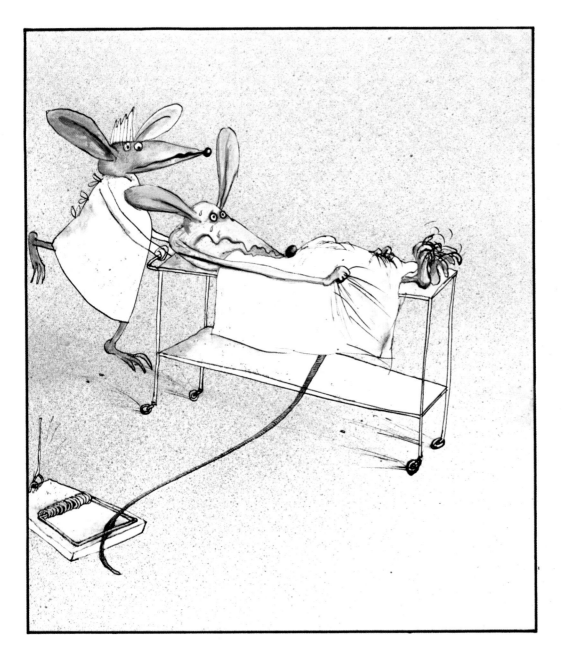

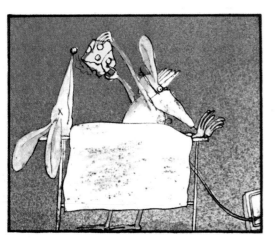

"Anaesthetic," Surgeon Mouse demanded, and Sister Mouse placed a large piece of cheese under Champion Mouse's nose. He fell asleep at once.

His tail was soon set free from the trap and put into splints.

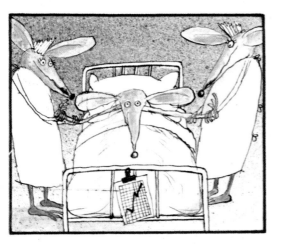

When he awoke he was back in his own bed, in the ward, and two Nursing Mice were holding his hands.

Champion Mouse recovered very quickly. He was impatient to go hunting along that cheese-trail again.

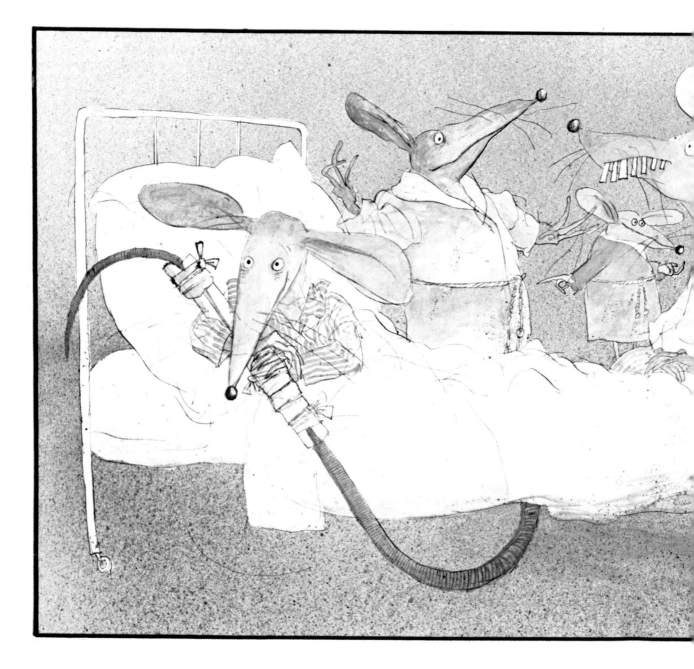

As the patients gathered around his bed, Champion Mouse suddenly said, "Shsh! I hear the sound of squeaky footsteps on the polished floor. It must be morning. Hurry, get all the beds back inside. I will make sure we have left everything neat and tidy."

Putting on his bright red tartan dressing-gown, he raced along the ward, but was stopped in his tracks by a huge noisy monster coming towards him.

He darted out of the way
only to run into a sweeping
brush that was leaning
against the wall.

He climbed up the brush
handle and as he reached the
window-sill, a gust of air
nearly blew him off again.
An electric-fan had been
switched on.

Then a radio was turned on and the noises confused him. He must escape before it was too late.

He slid down the broom handle, under the tea-trolley and around an oxygen cylinder.

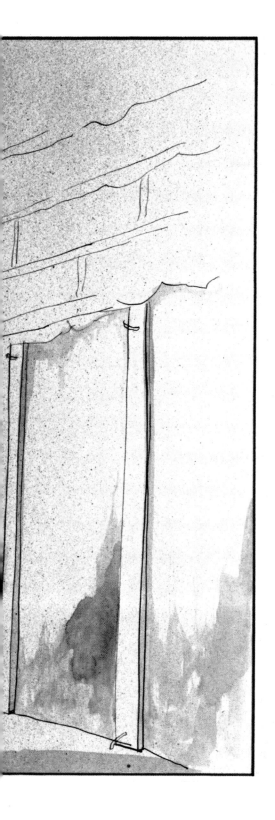

Breathlessly, he reached safety
and was once more back
behind the skirting board with
the other mice.

Henry awoke. The early dawn sunlight was shining through the avenue of trees outside the bay windows in front of him. He stretched, yawned, and sat up as a nurse came towards him pushing the early morning tea-trolley.

"Good morning, Henry. Did you sleep well?" she asked.

Henry glanced at the skirting-board, smiled, and answered, "Yes, thank you, nurse, I slept very well, very well indeed."

"That's good," she smiled, "because the doctor said you were better. Your mother phoned and sent her love. She will be coming to take you home today. I promised her that I would tell you straightaway that your white mouse is well again, too."